KU-626-205

A DEER
FROM THE
HILL

Other Hodder Story Books

FLYING LESSONS
Pippa Goodhart

THE LITTLE GREY DONKEY
Helen Cresswell

Other books by Maggie Pearson
for older readers

OWL LIGHT

DARK OF THE MOON

NIGHT PEOPLE

ALIEN DAWN

A DEER
FROM THE
HILL

Maggie Pearson

Illustrated by Jason Cockcroft

Hodder
Children's
Books

a division of Hodder Headline plc

Text copyright © 1999 by Maggie Pearson
Illustrations copyright © 1999 by Jason Cockcroft

First published in Great Britain in 1999
by Hodder Children's Books

The right of Maggie Pearson and Jason Cockcroft to be
identified as the Author and Illustrator of the Work has been
asserted by them in accordance with the Copyright,
Designs and Patents Act 1988.

10   9   8   7   6   5   4   3   2   1

All rights reserved. No part of this publication may be
reproduced, stored in a retrieval system, or transmitted, in any
form or by any means without the prior written
permission of the publisher, nor be otherwise circulated in any
form of binding or cover other than that in which it is published
and without a similar condition being imposed on the
subsequent purchaser.

All characters in this publication are fictitious and any resem-
blance to real persons, living or dead, is purely coincidental.

A Catalogue record for this book is available from the British
Library

ISBN 0340 73659 3

Printed and bound in Great Britain by
Clays Ltd, Bungay, Suffolk

For Liz -
'my little sister'

CONTENTS

CHAPTER ONE   11

CHAPTER TWO   20

CHAPTER THREE   35

CHAPTER FOUR   47

CHAPTER FIVE   59

CHAPTER SIX   72

CHAPTER SEVEN   86

A branch from the forest;
a fish from the river;
a deer from the hill:
these three are each man's right.

Highland proverb

Chapter One

PICTURE A LONG STRETCH
of water between high, craggy hills,
reflecting a heather-blue sky. A soft
breeze ruffles the surface, brushing
away the last, lazy cobwebs of morning mist.

On the far shore, shoulder to shoulder,
stands a dark army of pine-trees. But here,
behind us, the land is a crazy patchwork of
greys and purples and bracken-brown and
shades of green, with a raggle-taggle of low,
white houses. On this side stand two people,

a man and a child.

The child, booted and bobble-hatted and bundled up against the morning chill, could be a girl; might be a boy.

The man's hair is silvered and his skin is like fine leather. But he has a pair of legs on him still that would outstretch yours, over moor and mountain, and never mind the weather.

Pointing across the loch, the man says: 'Look there, just above the trees. Do you see the mist curling about the mouth of that cave, there? Like the smoke from a fire? We call that mist Young Donald's Fire.

'Long, long ago, so the story goes, Young Donald was a rebel, on the run from the English soldiers. One morning, early, they saw that mist, like smoke spiralling upwards and thought they'd got him cornered. By the time they'd sweated up to the cave in their lobster-red coats and discovered their mistake, Young Donald was long gone. Vanished away with the morning mist!

'When you see the smoke of Young Donald's Fire, that is always a sign it will be a fine day.

'Time we were off! We have a tidy walk ahead of us and I promised your mother we'd be there and back by tea-time. So: best foot forward! And I will tell you a story as we go along, to make the way seem shorter. No: it is not about Young Donald. Then again, it might be. It is mostly an adventure of my own, when I was roughly your age.'

He turns away, up the gravelled track, and the child tramps patiently after him.

'It was on a raw day in November (the man begins) that my father, your great-grandfather, was sent to prison.

You look surprised. Your mother never mentioned to you that we had had a jailbird in the family? I promise you this is a true story. Every word of it. Three months he got, and fined twenty-five pounds. That does not sound like much money nowadays, I know, but it was a lot to find then, for a man who was only on casual work, with a wife and a child to keep.

It was bitterly cold that November - though no snow yet, except on the highest mountain tops - and my father was going to be in prison for Christmas. The worst of it was, he had not been poaching the deer at all. Not that time. A man would have to be a fool, he said, to be after the deer there, on the far side of

14

the loch, under the pine trees. There is no grazing for them there at all. Mr Menzies, who was the Police, agreed with him. But he had to charge him, just the same, because of the witness against him and the holes in the boat.

This was the way it happened.

My father had taken the motorboat out along the loch, to see if he could get a bit of fish for supper. But the fish were not biting that day. So, after a while, he left his line and got in the dinghy that he towed behind the

boat and rowed himself across to the shallow waters on the far shore.

And he took his gun with him, because a gun is not something you leave lying about for anyone to find, even on a boat in the middle of the loch.

He got out of the dinghy (still carrying the gun) and went to stretch his legs, as he put it, where it was private, among the trees. It is always dark there, under the pines. The sun never shines and no birds sing. Your feet move so silently on the dead pine-needles, you might almost think yourself a ghost.

It was as he was turning back towards the loch, that he thought he saw a gleam of light, low down, where the shadows were darkest. Looking harder, the light seemed to be reflecting off a pair of polished army boots.

He rubbed his eyes. And then he was able to make out, above the boots, a pair of army trousers. Slowly, looking up and up, he could see the shape of a soldier, in full battle-gear, with a rifle under his arm, standing half-hidden behind a tree and perfectly still.

While my father was still wondering if what

he thought he could see was really there at all,
the soldier roused himself. He asked my
father what he thought he was doing there.

My father said he was minding his own
business.

'This is private property,' the soldier says
then.

My father answered him that, for as long as he could remember, he had been free to walk where he liked, so long as he did no damage.

'No damage!' The soldier nodded. 'Just to be on the safe side, I'd better be taking that.' He pointed to my father's gun.

'You will not,' says my father.

Then the soldier said he was arresting my father for a poacher.

My father was not a tall man to look at. Nor broad. But he was one of these people who are somehow bigger inside than out. He calmly looked that soldier up and down, rifle and great army boots and all. He said that, since he had been asked to leave, he would be going now. And he would be taking his gun with him.

Then he turned and walked away.

Silently the soldier followed him, the tramp-tramp-tramp of his army boots quite deadened by the pine-needles. But my father could tell he was matching him step-for-step, by the feel of the man's warm breath on his neck. Without once looking round, my father pushed the dinghy off from the shore.

18

The soldier might have stopped him then, before he could climb in and pick up the oars. But he was maybe too afraid of getting a drop or two of water on his beautiful, shiny boots.

Instead, as my father rowed away, he yelled, 'Come back!' and lifted his rifle and fired a shot - and then another - over my father's head.

Only an idiot will go towards a man who is firing a gun at him. My father kept on rowing away as hard as he could. Soon he was back on board the motorboat and starting her up.

He thought the soldier's gun must be empty by now. But what did this madman do but reload! And begin firing again, directly at the boat! The bullets tore into the wood low down, by the waterline. My father was not halfway across the loch before he had to stop the engine and bail for his life.

Twice more he had to do that before he was safe on the home shore.

Chapter Two

HE WAS ANGRY WHEN HE GOT home! Everyone knew that the Englishmen who had taken the Big House for the hunting season were determined to stop the poaching. But hiring armed soldiers, to fire real bullets, was taking things too far! He could have been drowned, he said, and the motorboat would cost a mint of money to repair. Aye, and he'd had to cut loose his fishing gear, too! He was going down to see Mr Menzies, the Police, first

20

thing in the morning.

But that same evening it was Mr Menzies who came round to us, to say the people from the Big House would be bringing charges.

'Charges!' my father exclaimed, and Mr Menzies (head and shoulders taller though he was), took a step or two backwards, out of harm's way. 'What charges? I've done nothing!'

'All the same, Iain,' says Mr Menzies, very quiet, very reasonable as always, which made him a hard man to argue with, 'I must ask you to hand over your gun.'

My father fetched the little gun, the .22, and Mr Menzies looked at it.

'Is this the gun?' he asked.

'That is my gun,' my father said.

Mr Menzies took it without another word, though he knew my father would have taken the .303 if he had been after the deer. It made no difference when the case came to court. Three months, they said, and fined twenty-five pounds. For doing nothing!

'And what about me?' my father demanded, 'What about the damage to my boat?'

They said the Englishman in his army boots had only fired at the boat so he would know it later, by the bullet holes, and that was all right for him to do. My father said loudly, for everyone to hear, including the local papers, that the Englishman might have known the boat again from the name Jeannie painted on it (which was the same as my mother's name, by the way), if he had only stayed in school long enough to learn to read. And if he had had enough brains to remember simple messages.

It did him no good. They took him away to prison and my mother's sister, Bea and Bea's friend Moira brought my mother home in Moira's car.

But that is not the end of my story. It is hardly even the beginning.

Shall we stop here a moment and catch our breath?

If you look back, you will see how high we have climbed already. There is the roof of the Big House, down among the trees, where the people lived who put my father in jail. There were always people coming and going, during the hunting season. Eager to stalk the deer and shoot the grouse and fish the salmon. So many different people, we never knew their names. All gone. No-one lives there now. Only the mice and the foxes and the birds building their nests in peace.

Shall we walk on? Try taking smaller steps when we come to the next steep bit and you won't get so out of puff.

So: there I was, waiting for my mother and father to come home from the courtroom that November afternoon. I'd lit the oil-lamps and made up the fire and set the kettle on the hob to boil and read the same page of my book ten times over without remembering a word of it, when I heard Moira's car outside.

I ran to the window and looked and saw the three women stepping out. No sign of my father at all.

They came in and sat themselves down at the table in the three places I'd laid for our tea. I sat alone, cross-legged on the rag-rug by the fire. Between them they told me what had happened.

'You will have to wait till next Christmas for the bike, Jamie, I'm afraid,' my mother said at last.

As if the Christmas money going to pay the fine was all that would be bothering me! I pictured those sheriff's men, like misers in a story-book, counting out all the sixpences and shillings and half-crowns it had taken my mother all year to save. I wished it had all been in pennies and half-pennies, so as to make it harder for them.

Auntie Bea made tea for three. Moira got out a quarter-bottle of whisky and poured a generous measure into each cup, which couldn't be doing much for the taste of the tea, or the whisky, to my mind. I wondered what my father would have to say about it, if he knew they were drinking whisky in his house at five o'clock in the afternoon.

But I sipped my warm milk and said nothing.

I listened.

I listened mostly to Moira, because she was always the one with most to say. She is still a woman with strong opinions on most things.

She goes to all the demos. A bit of a march and a demo afterwards is her idea of an afternoon well spent. She has sat down in front of police horses and chained herself to railings and lived in tree-houses and thrown things at men in expensive suits. She's a grand woman, is Moira.

'A deer is a pest,' she said, 'that will eat every bit of green in sight if you let it. Anyone may shoot a deer, if the deer is on his land. But what chance do you have of that, with a little bit of garden like yours? These English, now - ' (I knew she would come to the English sooner or later; it is always the English who are at the bottom of things, according to Moira) ' - these English, with their fat cheque-books, will buy up an estate of twenty thousand acres, rivers and mountain-tops and all. And it is only so they can swank about it to their posh friends in London. And they will say the deer belong to them, because the deer are more likely to be on their land than not. And they will put a poor man in prison only for carrying a gun. And take his savings off him, too.'

'It was different in the old days,' murmured Auntie Bea, feeling it was time someone else got a word in. 'Before the young laird went off to the war.'

'What was he thinking of?' sighed Moira.

'To go off and get himself killed like that, and leave us at the mercy of the English!'

I did not think she ought to be saying that. The young laird was our local hero. Mr Beaton had told us at school how the laird went off to fight in the war against the Germans, taking his piper with him to play him into battle. The piper marched up and down with his bagpipes, while men fell all around him - the young laird, too - and came off without a scratch.

The piper was *my* hero.

Moira said: 'The old laird knew where his duty lay. He lived on the estate. He knew the people. He gave work to them all. If there was a tile off the roof or a window broken, he would send a man to fix it the very same day. And the keeper would turn a blind eye, if an honest man went out to get a bit of meat for the pot.'

Myself, I doubted whether the old days had been so great that I would have liked to live in them. We had done the old days at school. Children walked barefoot to school if the weather was good, to save their one pair of shoes for the winter. With nothing but a baked potato in their pockets for dinner.

'In the old days,' said Moira, 'it was

A branch from the forest.
A fish from the river.
A deer from the hill.

That was a poor man's right.'

My mother protested gently that my father was not such a poor man as all that. And, by the way, he had not been out after the deer - not that time. But Moira was well into her stride by now.

'Iain should have fired back at that Englishman, while he was being shot at by him,' said Moira. 'It would have been in self-defence.'

I was thinking it was probably not such an easy thing to do, to steer a leaking boat with

one hand and fire a rifle behind you with the
other. My father was not some comic-book
hero.

'To let his gun be taken from him without
even firing a shot!' exclaimed Moira.

'They only took the .22,' my mother said.
'The .303 is still safe upstairs.'

'Is it now?' said Moira, suddenly turning
thoughtful.

'What are you thinking, Moira?' asked Auntie Bea.

'I am thinking,' said Moira, 'that they should pay for what they have done. For putting the man of the house in jail. For taking the money you had saved. And for the repairs to the boat.'

Then they noticed me there, listening, with the milk almost cold in the mug on my lap.

'Off you go, Jamie,' my mother said. 'Time for bed.'

It was not my bedtime. Nowhere near it. But I went. I kissed my mother and Auntie Bea and said goodnight to Moira. There was a look in her eye that I knew well. It is the look she still has when she's off on a Saturday with her Oxfam bag crammed with flour-bombs and a clutch of home-made banners tucked under her arm.

I lay in bed, wide awake, with my feather mattress fluffed up around me, snug as a bird in the nest. Downstairs, I could hear the women's voices, Moira's loudest and longest of the three.

I must have dozed for a while; when I

listened again, there was silence. You cannot imagine how quiet the nights were then. With no electricity, people went early to bed. There was no sound of televisions or cassette-players; no distant traffic (the main road was not built then); no talk from holiday-makers wandering back to their self-catering cottages from the hotel bar. Only the night-wind whispering and the ripple of the waters; the murmur of sheep on the hillside. Sometimes the cry of an owl, or the bark of a fox would jerk you awake.

It is a little like that up here. Up here, you can listen to the wind and hear the insects busy in the grass. You can almost imagine how it would be if we were the only two people left living in all the world. But a hundred years ago, or more, there would have been crofts, small farms, clusters of houses. They are all in ruins now. Deserted. But sometimes, when the light is right, you can still make out a haze of green, where oats and barley used to grow; the lines of kale and turnips; and the lazy-beds of potatoes. As if the land remembers.

There, on the hillside opposite, you can just see the shape of a township of six or seven houses. Why did the people leave? That is a sad, sad story.

In those days, the landlord's men could come and turn you out for any reason, or no

reason at all. If he needed more grazing for
his sheep - and there was more money to be
made out of sheep than out of people. If he
had a fancy to take up deer-hunting or
grouse-shooting, people would be in the way.
Out you would go. Without warning.
The landlord's men would come and tell you
to get out before they set fire to the thatch.
All you could do was snatch up the pots and
pans; the spinning-wheel; the blankets and
the fire-irons. Whatever you couldn't carry -
the furniture, the crops, the cloth half-woven
on the loom and the pans of milk half-turned
to cheese - all the rest had to be left behind.

It was Moira's great-grandfather who
snatched up a clod of earth as he went and
put it in his pocket, hoping that some day his
children might come back. Or their children.
Or their grandchildren.

Moira keeps it still, that little piece of earth,
in an old Oxo tin, on top of the kitchen
dresser. She says, if she had been there, she
would not have given up so easily. She
would have stood and fought them off, the
landlord's bullies.

A Deer from the Hill

Over the stepping-stones now. Don't worry; those rubber-soled boots of yours won't slip. Take hold of my crook and I'll pull you across. The water runs fast and fierce, but it's not deep. The worst that can happen to us is a bootful of ice-cold water, straight from the mountain-tops. There! Safely over. We'll make a highlander of you yet! On we go.

Chapter Three

IT WAS A FEW DAYS LATER, on the Friday evening. I'd finished my homework and was sitting with my book by the fire. My mother suddenly put down her sewing and asked whether I would mind if she went out that night for a while, with Auntie Bea and Moira.

Of course I didn't mind. I was quite big enough to be left. But she still fussed.

'I won't go till after you are in bed, so there will be no need to worry about switching things off, or banking up the fire, or locking up.'

I could have done all those things, if she had asked me. She knew I could. But I didn't argue.

It was long after I was in bed that I heard Moira's car draw up outside. But I went down again in my dressing-gown and slippers, to see my mother off and say: 'Have a nice time.'

She had not dressed up as she usually did for an evening out. She was wearing a pair of my father's old trousers; a thick sweater that made it hard to get her coat done up over it; and wellington boots, with woollen socks turned over the tops. When she heard me coming down the stairs, she gave a guilty start, as if she'd been a burglar, caught robbing her own house. Quickly she stuffed something into her pocket. But she was not so quick I didn't see it was my balaclava helmet.

'Jamie!' she said. 'What are you doing up?'

I said, 'I came to say goodbye. Have a nice time. Don't worry about me.'

'I won't,' she smiled. 'Not if I know
you're safe in bed. Off you go, now!'
   She watched me up the stairs.
   I turned round when I was halfway.
   'And off I go!' She said it cheerfully;
so why did she make me think of the story
Mr Beaton told us at school, of Captain

Oates going out to lose himself in the snow, so his friends would have a better chance of coming home alive?

I turned again at the top of the stairs and saw, as she closed the door, that she was carrying my father's gun, the .303.

And still I did not guess what they were up to, my mother and Moira and Auntie Bea. No; not even the next day when Auntie Bea came round with her mail order catalogue and my mother said I should have my new bike for Christmas after all.

'I can pay off the money week by week,' she said.

I did not think my father would be too keen on that idea. He always said you should save your money first, before you spent it. But what was I to do, with my mother looking so pleased to think she'd solved the problem, and all those bikes staring up at me from the pages of the catalogue, begging me to give them a home?

So I chose one.

You would not think much of it now, if you

could see it beside all these mountain bikes,
with their twelve-speed gears, so light you can
pick them up in one hand. But, to me, it was
a Rolls-Royce among bikes. It had three
speeds and a pump; a light on the front and a
dynamo on the back; a carrier; and a saddlebag with a tool-kit for mending punctures. I
thought I would be using that quite a bit,
because a lot of the roads round about were
just grit and pebbles.

And I chose the purple one,
not the red, because
it was a more
dignified sort of
colour.

Then I tried hard to forget about it, because
Christmas presents are supposed to be a
surprise.

It would be one in the eye for Murdo
Patterson, when he saw me with my new
bike. He didn't believe me when I told him,
back in September, that I was promised a
brand-new bike for Christmas. He would
have called me a liar to my face, and gone on
calling me it, if I had had no bike to show
him.

But he'd already found another way to tease
me. I suppose he got it from Anne Menzies.
She is a terrible gossip still. In those days
she would swap any secret she knew for a
half-share in a packet of Smarties. And she
knew a lot of secrets, because her father was
Mr Menzies, the policeman.

My father was a jailbird.

Once Murdo Patterson knew, the whole
school knew.

He would mutter to his cronies, when I was
just close enough to hear, things like: 'Hold
on to your sweetie-money, boys! Here comes

young Rob Roy to filch it off you.'

One day I fetched my coat to go home and found big arrows chalked all over it, like the clothes prisoners wear in the old silent movies. It was a terrible job to rub the marks off before my mother saw.

The word 'jail-bird' specially appealed to Murdo's gang. It saved them the trouble of thinking up clever things to say. All any of them had to do to fash me was whistle like a canary in a cage. The terrible thing about someone whistling behind your back is that it's very hard to know who is doing it.

I wished my father had been in prison for robbing a bank. Or smuggling diamonds. Or stealing the pictures out of some big museum. They would not have been so disrespectful then. But no: my father was doing three months for poaching. Except that he hadn't taken so much as a rabbit. That made it worse. That made him a fool as well as a jailbird.

The whistling turned to soft calls of 'Cuckoo! Cuckoo!'

I tried to keep my dignity, pretending I

didn't hear. But I knew there was only one way it could end.

Murdo was quite a lot bigger than me in those days. (He is not such a big man now and quite out of condition, after forty years of selling insurance.) The only way I would stand a chance in a fight with Murdo was to get one good blow in first.

So one day, at playtime, I kept my fist clenched ready for the sound of the 'Cuck-', close behind me. Before the '-oo', I'd spun round and hit him right on the nose.

Murdo was still looking surprised when he hit me back.

I would have been knocked clean over, if two of the others hadn't caught me and pushed me back into the fray.

Then we were at it, hammer and tongs.

Murdo was big, but I was angry. It was Murdo who was on the ground, with me on his chest and his blood, not mine, scattered all around, when Mr Beaton came out to see what the row was about and hauled me off by my collar.

Murdo, blood streaming from his nose, told Mr Beaton I had started it.

I told him it was Murdo's fault. It was an affair of honour. I was defending my father's good name as well as my own. But Mr Beaton was a city man, from Inverness, who did not understand these things. He said we were both to stay indoors at playtime for a week, where he could keep an eye on us.

I didn't mind. I would rather be indoors reading a book, than out in the cold, trying to find something to do for a quarter of an hour. The classroom windows were so high up, you could see nothing out of them but a little piece of the sky. And with the beams criss-crossing the ceiling above, if I turned my back on the desks and chairs and huddled close to the stove, it was easy to imagine myself aboard the Hispaniola, sailing through tropical seas to Treasure Island; or in some old castle, with my lord Ivanhoe lying wounded, and me his loyal side-kick, guarding him with my life.

Murdo didn't read books. He spent most of those playtimes sharpening pencils down to the stubs, or poking holes in bits of paper. I think he was always a bit afraid that if he used his brain too much, he'd wear it out before he was much older.

His nose bled for the rest of the morning. He soaked his own handkerchief and Mr Beaton's; then Mr Beaton sent him to lie down on the floor in the study. We didn't see

Murdo again until dinner was almost over. There was nothing left for him to eat but a bit of cold shepherd's pie and three Brussels sprouts that Mrs Ginelli, who did the dinners, had been going to give to the cat.

Mrs Ginelli, who didn't know about the fight and the nosebleed, stood over Murdo while he ate it. She said it would teach him to come in for his dinner on time in future.

There was nothing for his pudding but some custard, with thick skin on top.

'I don't like skin,' said Murdo.

'Eat it!' she said. And he did. I knew Murdo would find a way to get even with me if he could.

Chapter Four

THEN MY BIKE ARRIVED AND
that was enough to put any worries
about Murdo Patterson right out of
my head.

It didn't come with the postman. It came
in a great, big furniture-van thing that had
to go half a mile further up the glen before
it could find room to turn round. Then
back it came again. By this time, all the
neighbours who were at home had found
themselves an excuse to come out and take

a look. I never saw so many people sweeping doorsteps, dusting window-ledges and putting things in dustbins all at the same time.

That evening Moira came round with her toolbox to see that the bike was all fitted together and in working order. I was supposed to keep out of the way, but I peeped into the kitchen just long enough to see that they had sent the red one after all.

And I knew straight away that red was the colour I had wanted all along.

When Auntie Bea came round to collect the first payment, my mother went to the Chinese biscuit jar with the loose lid that always made the biscuits go soft, where we used to keep the Christmas money, and fetched out a one-pound note. She gave it to Auntie Bea with a look on her face as if she was happy to be giving money away.

'I'm sorry I've no change,' she said. 'You'd better take the pound, Bea. It will be paid off that much sooner.'

While she was seeing Auntie Bea to the door, I looked inside the Chinese jar and saw a neat little roll of paper money, done up with a rubber band - no coins at all. It had been nearly all coins before - before the money was taken to help pay my father's fine.

And still I did not guess what they were up to, my mother and Moira and Auntie Bea.

In those days, you see, there was man's work and there was woman's work. The man went out and earned the money and his wife stayed home and cooked and kept house. There was enough of that to do, with no elecricity for a washing machine, or a vacuum cleaner, or a deep-freeze, most of the food-shops ten miles away and only cold running water.

So, if it ever crossed my mind what she must be up to, going out after dark, in scruffy old clothes, with the .303 tucked under her arm, I would have told myself that I had been reading too many adventure books.

Then it was Christmas and I was allowed to have my new bicycle at last.

I had other presents, too, of course: socks and handkerchiefs and a set of coloured pencils; a new pullover my mother had knitted for me on the quiet; a model boat my father had made in the prison workshop; and a whole stack of books that Moira had grubbed out of the second-hand shops for me.

But, oh! that bicycle! With its matching pump and its three-speed gears and the light on the front and the dynamo on the back and

the saddlebag and the carrier - all just as the catalogue had promised.

The pride of riding it down to the village on Christmas morning!

The look on Murdo's face!

Every day of the holidays, I was out on that bike. Every day - twice! three times a day! - I was looking for errands to run. My mother

only had to say she thought she might be
getting a bit short of sugar and I'd be offering
to go and fetch some more, and handing her
her purse before she could say no.

If there were no messages to fetch, I rode to
the shop and back anyway, at least once a day,
just on the off-chance of getting another look
at Murdo's face.

I rode till I was saddle-sore, and it was
almost a relief when I got my first puncture.
I mended it myself, crouching by the front
step with the instructions open beside me and
my hands almost freezing as I turned the
inner tube round and round in a bowl of
water to find where the hole was. Then I
marked it, with the chalk provided. Dried it.
Patched it. Eased the tyre back on the wheel
again and pumped it up. It took me nearly
an hour. I soon learned to fix them more
quickly. But none of them was as much fun
as the first.

December had been bitterly cold, and January
was colder. Too cold for snow, people said. I
could never understand why they said that; in

the Arctic it must be colder still and there is
snow everywhere.

Still the three women were going out
together, once or twice a week. The roads
were icy, but that never seemed to bother
Moira.

I used to listen for the car driving off,
sliding a little as it turned the corner at
the bottom of the hill, then struggling to
straighten itself again, before I went to sleep.

If I woke sometimes when they came back,
it was because of the brightness of the head-
lights moving across the ceiling; they were
careful never to make a noise. So I was
surprised one night to be woken by the sound
of car doors slamming and heavy footsteps
outside.

Then came a loud knocking at the front
door.

I put on my dressing-gown and slippers and
went to open it.

I was careful. I put the chain on first, and I
was glad I had. There stood Mr John Brown,
who used to lord it over the estate while the
owners were away in England.

'Good evening, young man!' says he, acting all bluff and hearty. 'I'd like a word with your mother, if she's at home.'

'She is not at home,' I said. 'She is out with some friends.'

'Has she left you all alone in the house?'

'If she has had to leave me in the house alone,' I said, 'it is because you put my father in prison.'

'All the same,' he said, 'she might have got a baby-sitter in.'

I said, 'We have no money for a baby-sitter. Besides, I am not a baby any more.'

Then another man moved into the light from the doorway. An Englishman, by his voice. 'No money for a baby-sitter,' he said. 'But plenty for a nice, new bike!'

I felt my fingers suddenly lock tight round the edge of the door. For a whole minute - but it seemed like much, much longer - I forgot to breathe. It was not so much what the man said that had startled me, but seeing how he was dressed, like a soldier, with great, big army boots. The man the people up at the Big House had brought in

54

to get rid of the poachers. The man who had almost killed my father.

I understood at last what they had been up to, my mother and Moira and Auntie Bea.

They had been taking the deer from the estate and selling them.

And Mr John Brown had been asking about, to find out who had more money to spend than they ought to have.

'I suppose it was Murdo Patterson who told you about the bike,' I said in a wee, small voice. 'He is as green and sour as a June apple over that bike. My mother was nearly a whole year saving up for it.'

'In that case, if I could just have a word with her,' Mr John Brown said then, 'we can clear things up. Tonight, maybe? I don't suppose she'll be much longer, will she? Shall we come in and keep you company till she comes home?'

Then I was glad of the chain on the door.

'No, thank you,' I said. 'I must go back to bed now, ready for school in the morning. Goodnight, Mr Brown.'

I tried to close the door, but the other man had put his big army boot in the way. So I went to the kitchen and fetched a saucepan and a wooden spoon. There were still some lights showing in the houses nearby. I knew, from playing this game when I was little, that a dozen people were bound to hear me if I banged the saucepan loud enough with the spoon - and at least half of them would come over to tell me to stop.

When Mr John Brown
saw what I meant to do,
he signed to the other
man to take his foot
away, so I could close
the door.

They went back
to their car, but
they didn't drive
away. They sat
there, waiting, with
the lights turned off.

I watched them from
the upstairs window.

I thought if my mother came home while
they were there, she would be caught red-
handed. She would be sent to prison, like my
father. I would be a kind of orphan and sent
to that place in Oliver Twist, where they feed
you nothing but some horrible stuff called
gruel, and not enough of that.

An hour later the car was still there, and all
the neighbours in their beds.

How long would it be before the women
came back?

Another hour? Not much more. An hour before Moira's car came chugging up the track and she spotted the other car lying in wait, too late for her to turn round. And driving backwards was not what Moira was best at; she said retreat was not in her nature.

What should I do? Warn them, of course. How? I didn't know which way they had gone, except that I thought I remembered hearing the car turn left at the foot of the hill.

Besides, if I went to warn them, Mr John Brown and that soldier-fellow were sure to see me and follow.

That gave me an idea.

Chapter Five

QUICKLY I DRESSED MYSELF.
I crept downstairs in the dark and
let myself out the back way. I
took my bike from the lean-to we
grandly called the wash-house,
from its having the copper-boiler in, where
my mother used to boil the sheets and other
whites on Mondays. I pushed the bike round
to the front corner of the house.

There I stopped, to make sure the men had
seen me, before I set off, up the hill, not

down it, pushing my bike, with the lights still off, until I got to the corner. There I switched the lights on, front and back, as if I thought I must be out of sight by now. I got on and rode a little way, then stopped.

Would they take the bait?

When I had almost given up hope, I heard the car start up. They had been arguing, probably, about whether they should take the car, or save their legs. They must think I was really stupid, not to hear it and know I was being followed.

I took my time, pedalling uphill. I could tell, by the groaning of the engine, they were trying so hard not to catch me up, they were nearly rolling backwards.

I turned off, down a rough track, with deep ruts frozen hard and rocks sticking up, which must have given them a bumpy ride. Then off again, along a deer-path, where I knew the car could not go.

I stopped again and heard doors slam and voices carried on the clear night air. Behind me, through the frozen, criss-cross tracks of animals and birds, wound the clear, mazey trail of a bicycle wheel that would be too tempting for them not to carry on the chase.

But under the cover of the trees, where the frost had not formed, I would lose them easily, leave them blundering around in the dark, and make my way home.

That was my plan.

But this was not the plain, pine plantation where the trees grow straight with nothing in between. This wood, they say, is a little bit left over from the Great Caledonian Forest that was here before time began. The path twisted and turned beneath oaks and birch and rowan and hazel, with banks of briars and ivy clustering thick between. And no choice but to follow it.

The moon kept winking at me through the bare branches overhead, as if it knew something I didn't. Each patch of moonshine only made the shadows darker, shifting and growing as I passed.

From books I had read (and wished I hadn't!) I knew this was the lair of the pookah, who will leap out in the shape of a great black horse or dog, with eyes like glowing coals, and turn your hair white with fright. The brollachan, that is more fearsome still, since it has no shape at all. The kelpie that will leap up on to a lone rider's back and cling and cling until it has ridden him to his doom.

It was a relief to stop now and then and listen for the human sounds of Mr John Brown and his soldier-friend blundering through the woods behind me. They were trying to go quietly, but they had no talent at all for stalking. The more they shushed one another, tripping over stray roots and catching their heads on the branches, the more noise they made.

But now I had to lose them.

Up and down the woodland trails I went,
until I had quite lost myself. And still they
were there behind me. I got off my bike and
pushed it, thinking the rattling as I rode along
might be the reason they were still following.
It was a long, long time before I realised they
must be able to see the little red reflector light
on the back mudguard. Quickly I rubbed
some dirt on my handkerchief and tied it over
the top.

I hurried on, towards a place where I could
see the trees thinning out. There I would be
able to take a look around and get some idea
of where I was. As I came closer, peering
between the last of the trees, I could make out
stone walls, pale and frosted in the moonlight.

Houses!

I couldn't believe it; I must have gone
round in a circle and brought my two hunters
back to my own front door.

But it was worse than that; much worse.

A shudder ran through me, when I saw the
place I had come to. All the monsters that
had been jostling inside my head, which of
them could scare me most, shrank back to

story-book size and went off to sulk in a corner.

I had come to the abandoned township that I showed you, back there on the hillside. Do you remember? Where the people were all turned out by the cruel landlord, and their houses burned behind them. A haunted place. With real-life ghosts.

There were brothers and uncles of my friends at school who would swear they had been up here and, through the evening mist, heard the women crying and the shouts of the landlord's bullies; smelt the burning thatch!

And there was more than one hill-walker at dusk, who'd been aiming for our village by the loch and thought he'd reached it sooner than expected. The roofs were on the houses, he said, and the regular clickety-clack of the weaving looms coming from inside. The crops stood tall in the fields and the people were going quietly about their business, though none of them seemed to see him at all, or hear him when he spoke to them.

Now I came to think about it, the walls did seem taller than ever they looked by daylight. White walls, frozen in the moonlight, with doorways of a velvety blackness that would swallow you up and leave not a shadow behind. Frost sparkled everywhere, clustering on round boles of moss, turning them to dead men's skulls, thrusting out of the earth.

What was I to do? The tangle of undergrowth ran unbroken either side. Behind me, the men were coming closer. For a moment I was ready to turn round, give myself up and beg them to take me home.

Somehow, I found myself crouching in the shadow of a ruined wall, with a tree growing out of the stones spreading its leafless branches above. I thought it might be a rowan tree. The rowan would protect me against ghosts and shadows and things that went bump in the night.

I suddenly heard the men's voices. They were standing so close, if the wall had not been there, I could have touched them.

'We've lost him,' said Mr John Brown.

'Lost him?' the other man scoffed. 'We'll soon flush him out of there.'

Then Mr John Brown - I imagined him shaking his head - 'He won't have come here; they're afraid of this place. The children, especially.'

'He's here!' says the soldier.

Mr John Brown was an educated man, but still a local man; he'd heard the stories that were told when he was just a wee, small boy. 'We'll go back,' he said. 'And wait in the car.' Suddenly he caught his breath: 'Did you hear that?'

'What?'

'It sounded like a woman's voice.'

A woman's voice? Oh, no!

'Then we've got them!' says the soldier.

Oh no! My heart was thumping like a
signal drum *- no! no! no! -* and my breath
sounded as loud to me as the wind in a
chimney. Let it not be my mother and Moira
and Auntie Bea, after all I had done to save
them!

'No!' Mr John Brown said the word aloud.
'It was a woman weeping that I heard.' His
voice was trembling. 'Can you smell smoke?'

'Smoke?'

'Like heather thatch burning?'

'No,' said the soldier, sounding puzzled.

'All the same,' said Mr John Brown, 'I think we should go back.'

Then the soldier gave a shout: 'Look! There he goes!'

'Who?'

'The boy!'

What boy? Not me; they were not looking in my direction, but upward. Up the mountainside.

They went racing away up the path. From where I sat I could see them.

And I will tell you this, which I have never told another living soul. It was no stray deer, nor a sheep, nor a goat that I saw flitting ahead of them, away and up the mountain.

It *was* a boy! A barefoot, ragged boy, with tangled red hair down to his shoulders, who seemed to be laughing as he led them up, up, up and away from me. I could not hear him, but I saw him as clearly as I see you now. And it was no boy I had ever seen before or have seen since.

And as the three of them vanished into the shadows above me, the walls that had seemed so stiff and cold - and alive! - seemed to be settling themselves to snug sleep again.

I knew it was safe to go home.

I pushed my bike down one of the old deer-trots to the road. Moira passed me, coming the other way, as I was cycling home. She flashed her lights, but didn't stop; as if it was the most natural thing in the world to see a boy out on his bike at what must have been three o'clock in the morning.

'Where have you been, Jamie?' my mother exclaimed, as I came in from putting my bike away in the wash-house.

'Turn out the lights,' I said, 'Get into your night-clothes. Mr John Brown will be knocking on the door any minute.'

But it was a lot longer than that before they gave up chasing my barefoot, red-headed, ghostly friend and found their way back down the mountainside in the dark.

I heard my mother at the door: 'My son is in bed, Mr Brown. Where else would he be at this time of night? Yes, I have been out with some friends. No, I will not give you their names, for you to go knocking on their doors in the middle of the night. If you have anything more to ask me, please come back at a respectable time in the morning.'

But she had had a fright. She never went out again late at night with Moira and Auntie Bea. 'Jamie,' she said, 'I really don't think I am cut out for a life of crime.'

I was glad. I didn't want to be sent to that place where Oliver Twist went.

'Besides,' she said, 'there is plenty in the Chinese jar now to keep us going until your father comes home.'

Chapter Six

W E WERE NEVER A GREAT
family for kissing and
hugging, or even saying
very much. When my father
came home from prison, my mother's
welcome was to cook a big joint of beef for
dinner, though it was only Tuesday.

Myself, I was impatient to show him my
new bike.

'How have you been managing?' my father
asked.

'Well enough,' said my mother.

My father looked again at the new bike and the joint of beef on the table. He lifted the lid of the Chinese jar and peered inside. His pride was hurt, as man of the house, to think of his wife out earning the money. He said only two words: 'Oh, Jeannie!'

She stood, twisting the tea-towel in her hands. 'It is just the money that was taken for the fine. And to keep us while you were away. There should be enough left over to pay for mending the boat.'

It was left to me to explain. 'She has not been out working at all. They have been taking the deer. *A branch from the forest. A fish from the river. A deer from the hill.* That is the poor man's right, so Moira says.'

'It was Moira's idea,' my mother said. 'And a good one, too. She said the estate should pay. She told us the way to do it. You know how, when the weather is cold, like this, the deer come down close to the road at night, to feed. Well, Moira would drive along slowly, and I would shine the flashlight out of the window until we could see the glitter of their eyes. And I would fix on one, so it would be dazzled by the light, caught in the beam. Then Bea would shoot it. I would not have let her use your gun, if it had not been easiest for her to do from that side of the car, since she is left-handed.' Briskly she shook out the tea-towel. 'It was easy.'

'Easy!' my father said.

'Bea is a good, clean shot,' she said. 'The deer did not suffer at all.'

My father said nothing.

My mother carefully draped the tea-towel to dry, over the rack above the stove: 'I always cleaned the gun afterwards, as good as new.'

'Well,' said my father, sitting himself down at the table, 'it is a good piece of beef.'

It would be a pity to let it get cold.'

So my mother and I sat down too and we had our dinner.

The Saturday morning after that was the coldest day of the winter. It had snowed properly by then, and frozen, then snowed again. But the wind blew so, there were still places up among the rocks and gullies where no snow lay at all.

The cold and the wind never bothered my father. He would not stand out in a draught when he could come in; but if there was work that had to be done outside, weather was weather, what could you do?

For a while after breakfast he stood outside the door, staring up at the clouds, the way they tumbled and changed shape; then down at the loch and the pattern the waves made on the water. Then he nodded to himself - once, twice - and came back in and said to me: 'Put on your warmest clothes. Today I will show you the proper way to take the red deer.'

We drove for a while in the battered ex-Post Office van that was the only car my father ever owned. (One day, years later, as he was driving down the new motorway at his top speed of thirty-five miles an hour, the whole floor fell out of it and his driving days were over.) But that is another story.

When he stopped the van and I opened the door to get out, the cold wind sucked the breath right out of me, as if we had just landed on the moon. My father stood calmly studying the sky again and the faintest changes in the wind, almost as if he could smell the deer a mile off, as easily as they can scent a man. He knew their tracks; the places where they would go for shelter.

The deer can tell what the weather is going to do, better than those Met office men in London. Long before the storm clouds gather, they will be moving down from the high ground.

This path we are following now, was made by the deer. Walkers often use these tracks and never know it is the deer they have to thank for finding out the easiest way to go from glen to glen and up and down the steepest slopes.

At last my father set off, with his .303 in his hand, and a sack and a coil of rope over his shoulder. And I followed him, along footpaths and deer-tracks and over rough, rocky places where I could see no path at all. My father seemed to find his way by signs that were invisible to me, turning suddenly to left or right, or dropping downhill again when we had struggled almost to the top.

My body was warm enough. I was wearing so many jumpers, I looked like the Michelin man. But my toes were going stiff inside my wellingtons. I thrust my hands deep into my pockets, because woollen gloves did not keep out the bitter wind. I ended up with a chilblain right on the tip of my nose, in spite of my balaclava helmet.

Then, suddenly, 'Down!' my father mouthed at me, half-signalling with his hand, half-pulling me after him. I found myself lying on my stomach among the icy rocks, with snow creeping into my right boot.

I crawled after him, to the top of the ridge, peeped over and saw them grazing in a place where the snow-cover was thin and patchy, not a stone's throw away.

The red deer.

So beautiful they were, lifting their heads now and then to look, listen and sniff the air for the least hint of danger. One, in particular, I remember, seemed to know we were there. She kept high-stepping first one way, then the other. Then she would stop and give a sound between a cough and a bark. The others would glance up, listen, sniff the air, then seem almost to shrug their shoulders, and go back to nibbling the grass.

She was not the one my father had in his sights, as he steadied his arm on a slab of

rock, put the stock to his shoulder and laid his head against it. She was too skittish.

Once more she gave that coughing bark and this time they all stopped eating and stood, as if - too late! - they had understood the danger, just as he squeezed the trigger.

The bang made me jump. The deer took off, all at once, as if they were in a race. I thought the shot had missed, and I was glad.

Then, in mid-flight, one pulled up, finishing with a funny little dance step; fell; and never moved again. The rest ran on, heads tossing, tiny feet kicking up the snow, over the rocky ridge and down the other side and out of sight.

We were alone again, myself, my father and the poor, dead deer.

I stayed where I was while my father went down with his knife to see to it. It is a messy business; not something you want to hear about. At last he wrapped the sack he had brought around his shoulders, lifted the carcass up and tied it with the rope.

He was not a tall man, or a broad one, but he was strong. He carried that deer, the weight of a sack of potatoes, all the way back to the van, without once stopping to rest. We took the quickest way this time and it was mostly downhill, but it must have been two miles at least, and over rough ground.

'And that is the proper way to take the red deer,' he said, as he tumbled it into the van and slammed the door behind it. 'The man who has tracked the deer and killed it with one clean shot and carried it back on his own two shoulders is the man who has a right to it.'

So we drove home and my father left me there for my mother to thaw out by the fire, while he went on to the butcher's shop in town. When he came back, he brought a fine, big piece of venison - deer-meat - for our dinner.

My mother looked at it long and hard. Then she said: 'Do you remember when we went to see the film about the young deer, Bambi? How Jamie and I cried when Bambi's mother was killed by the huntsmen? When we were out taking the deer, I never once saw one fall without thinking of Bambi's mother.

I will cook the venison for you and Jamie, but I shall not be able to eat a mouthful of it.'

Then I looked at it, too. I knew it was not a piece of the same deer I had seen alive one minute and dead the next, up on the mountain. Venison must be hung a good week or ten days before it is fit to be eaten. But I knew I could not eat a morsel of it either. No, not even to please my father.

He looked from one to the other of us:

'The deer must be culled,' he said. 'The weak and the old will die anyway before the cold weather is over. It is a kindness to kill them now, quickly, and leave more grazing for the rest. And once the beast is dead, why shouldn't we eat it?'

But he could not persuade us.

He shook his head: 'You two!' he said.

Then he picked up the venison and went out again. We heard the van drive off. When he came back, it was a parcel of an altogether different shape that he put down on the table. He had swapped that piece of venison for a fine, fat salmon.

'You would not eat the deer from the hill,'

he said. 'So here is a fish from the river.
Now throw another branch from the forest
on the fire, and let's eat!'

Very good it was, too. I cannot be
sentimental about fish, though they are
beautiful, too, in their way.

On our way back, I will show you the
waterfall, where the salmon leap upstream -
though you will have to come back again at
the end of the summer to see them.

I will teach you how to catch a salmon with your bare hands. To slip both hands under him and twist your whole body round and up, so you flip him clear of the water!

At this time of the year they are swimming downstream, towards the sea and the ocean. Years they will spend away - no-one knows where exactly - but sooner or later they will always come back to the place where they were born, swimming against the current, leaping up waterfalls twice the height of a man, forgetting even to eat.

Sometimes people find themselves drawn back, too. A man came all the way from Canada last year, looking for his roots. The land his family had left, over a hundred years ago. Wherever I took him, he said he felt as if he knew the place already; as if he had come home.

At last I took him up to the old ruined township and told him the story, how the people were turned off their land to make way for the landlord's flock of sheep.

He was a good man. A kind man. I did not have the heart to tell him what I knew as soon as he told me his name; that his great-grandfather was the landlord's man who turned the people out and burned their homes behind them.

Chapter Seven

I WENT OUT OFTEN WITH MY
father after that day I saw him shoot
the deer. He taught me everything he
knew about the creatures of woodland
and moor and mountain. The fox, the red
squirrel, the wildcat and the mountain hare.
The osprey and the capercaillie. Best of all,
I loved the stalking of the deer. Running with
my back bent parallel to the ground, mile
upon mile; threading the seams of a bog;
or gliding down the bed of a burn on my

stomach; learning how to make use of every scrap of cover, heather and rocks and bracken, in snow or sleet or frost; and not to mind the biting of the midges.

They say the stag is monarch of the glen. But it is the midges that drive him out of the glen in summer and up to the high pastures. So, who is king of the castle then?

The pleasure for me was always in the stalking; never in the kill. My father never understood that; but he never shot another deer when I was with him.

'You have done well today, for a beginner. The story helped, did it?

'The way back will be shorter. We have had to come round the long way, so as to get down-wind, where the deer cannot catch our scent. We have the sun behind us, too; which is good.

'Do you want to stop now, for a bite to eat? Or shall we go on, now we are so close?'

The child looks at him and says nothing. If you had a penny for every word that child spoke, you'd be lucky to be a pound the richer come Friday. But the man understands.

'We'll go on then. Has it been a good day so far?'

The child nods. If it nodded any harder, it would nod its head right off.

'The best bit is still to come. Do you know

how to stand still as a statue? No fidgetting?
Quiet as a mouse? Deer are shy creatures, but
inquisitive. If you are patient, they may come
to you, close enough to touch.

'Just over the next ridge, I think, we will
see them. We must not show ourselves
against the sky. Keep your head down, until
we have that big rock over there behind us.
Do as I do.'

Slowly the two of them edge upwards
and along, clothes, brown and green and
grey, slowly fading into the colours of the
landscape.

If they would only look back once - just once!
They would see, watching, on the slope below
them, a boy. A barefoot, red-headed, silently
laughing boy in ragged clothes.

Young Donald watches them till they are
out of sight; then turns away and down the
glen towards the hillside opposite and the

township of six or seven heather-thatched houses, with smoke curling from the chimneys. The distant clatter of the looms mingles with the hum of insects in the grass; and the crops are standing tall in the fields all around.

Then the sun comes out from behind a cloud, a sudden breath of wind sighs down from the cold mountain-tops, scattering the last shreds of morning mist, and there is nothing after all but a cluster of ruined walls and the memory of green fields.

FLYING LESSONS

"Arms by his sides, up on tiptoe and leaning forward, Duncan flapped his wings."

Duncan can't even fly the length of the aviary on his chick-sized wings. He's left behind with all the little fledgelings while his friends have long since taken to the skies.

Suddenly, the wild marches are an appealing prospect, however dangerous.
Somewhere he can be alone with the wild birds and master the art of flying.
Before long, his biggest problem could be how to get back down to earth . . .

h **HODDER** Another Story Book from Hodder Children's Books

THE LITTLE GREY DONKEY

*"A donkey knows her own master, Pietro,
and to her you are only a friend."*

When Pietro's grandfather is taken into
hospital he can no longer keep up his
vegetable deliveries. Pietro promises to help.

But Pietro hadn't bargained on his
grandfather's obstinate little donkey,
Modestine. How can he make his deliveries if
Modestine won't obey him? And if he can't
keep up the deliveries, how will his family pay
the hospital fees?

Amanda, Pietro's new American friend,
has her own special way of dealing with
his problems - and sets the whole town
in uproar . . .

0 340 722 444	FLYING LESSONS *Pippa Goodhart*	£3.50	☐
0 340 70451 9	THE LITTLE GREY DONKEY *Helen Cresswell*	£3.50	☐

All Hodder Children's books are available at your local bookshop or newsagent, or can be ordered direct from the publisher. Just tick the titles you want and fill in the form below. Prices and availability subject to change without notice.

Hodder Children's Books, Cash Sales Department, Bookpoint, 39 Milton Park, Abingdon, OXON, OX14 4TD, UK. If you have a credit card you may order by telephone. Our call centre team would be delighted to take your order. Our direct line is 01235 400414 (lijnes open from 9.00am to 6.00 pm Monday to Saturday, 24 hour message answering service). Alternatively you can send a fax on 01235 400454.

Or please enclose a cheque or postal order made payable to Bookpoint Ltd to the value of the cover price and allow the following for postage and packing: UK & BFPO - £1.00 for the first book, 50p for the second book, and 30p for each additional book ordered up to a maximum charge of £3.00.
OVERSEAS & EIRE - £2.00 for the first book, £1.00 for the second book, and 50p for each additional book.

Name ....

Address ....
....
....
....

If you would prefer to pay by credit card, please complete:

Please debit my Visa/ Access/ Diner's Club/ American Express (delete as applicable) card no:

Signature ....
Expiry Date ....